D1380152

# Lincolnshire
## COUNTY COUNCIL

## discover libraries

**This book should be returned on or before the due date.**

To renew or order library books please telephone 01522 782010
or visit https://lincolnshire.spydus.co.uk

You will require a Personal Identification Number.
Ask any member of staff for this.

**The above does not apply to Reader's Group Collection Stock.**

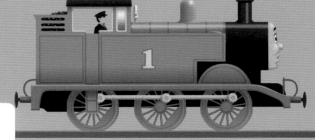

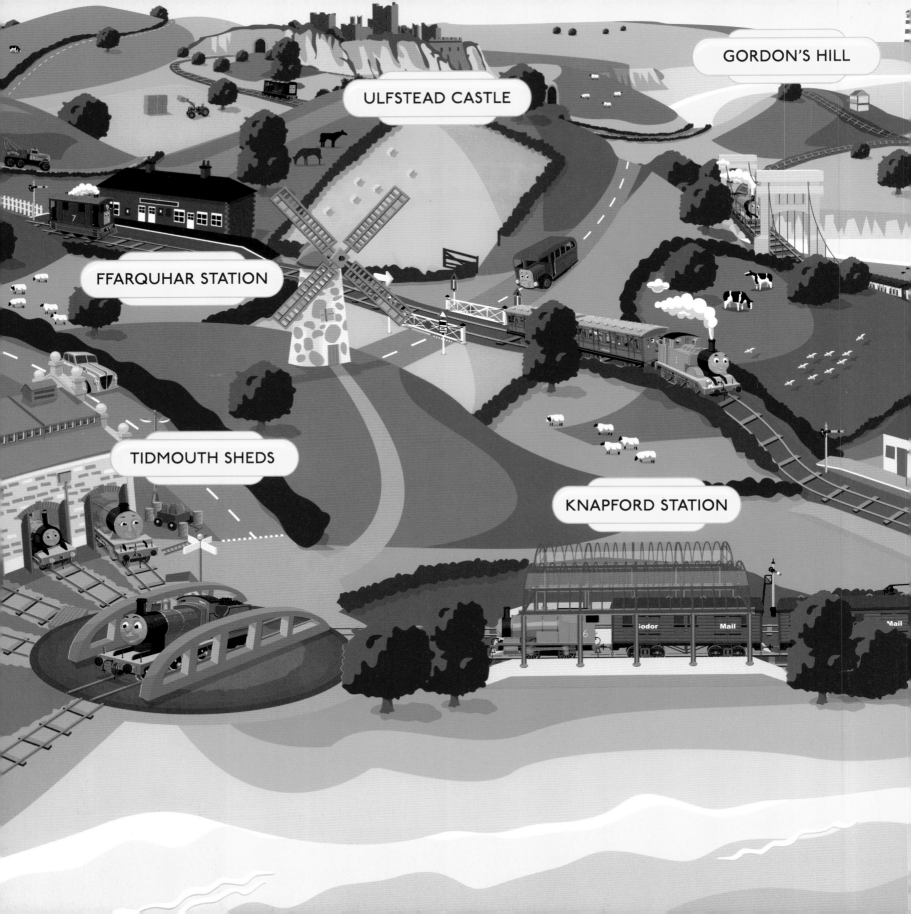

GORDON'S HILL

ULFSTEAD CASTLE

FFARQUHAR STATION

TIDMOUTH SHEDS

KNAPFORD STATION

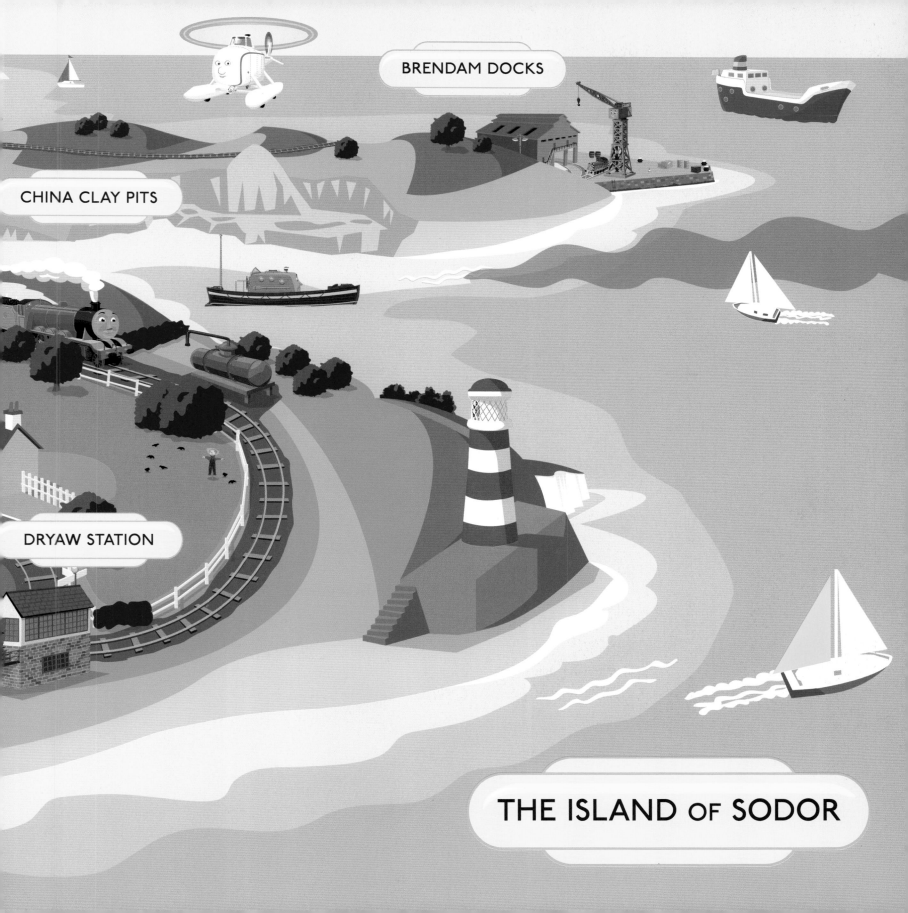

CHINA CLAY PITS

BRENDAM DOCKS

DRYAW STATION

THE ISLAND OF SODOR

# EGMONT

*We bring stories to life*

First published in Great Britain in 2020 by Egmont UK Limited
2 Minster Court, London EC3R 7BB

Written by Jane Riordan. Designed by Richie Hull and Rob Jones
Illustrated by Robin Davies  Map illustration by Dan Crisp

 Thomas the Tank Engine & Friends ™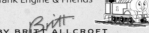

HiT entertainment    CREATED BY BRITT ALLCROFT

ISBN 978 1 4052 9675 5

70821/003

Printed in Poland


Egmont takes its responsibility to the planet and its inhabitants
very seriously. We aim to use papers from well-managed forests
run by responsible suppliers.

Stay safe online.
Egmont is not responsible for content hosted by third parties.

# Thomas the Hero

This is the story of when Thomas the Tank Engine discovered that you don't have to fly high to be a hero.

Thomas the Tank Engine was going about his work, as usual, when he heard a high-pitched, whistling sound up in the sky.

**"Whatever can that be?"** he said to himself.

Thomas looked up and saw a small plane darting overhead. He had never seen anything like it before.

**"Peep! Peep!"** called Thomas, but the plane didn't hear him.

The plane was soon out of sight.

"I must find out about that **flying machine,**" Thomas said to himself.

That night, in the Engine Sheds, Thomas asked James and Percy if they had seen anything flying overhead that day.

**"We keep our eyes fixed on the tracks,"** they said. "That way, we're **Really Useful Engines.**"

The next day, Thomas was determined to be a Really Useful Engine, but he couldn't help looking up for the plane.

He was just thinking that he'd never see it again when he heard that same whistling sound.

**Wwwweeeeeeee ......**

This time he just had to follow it ...

The plane may have been small, but it was fast.

"**Must keep up, must keep up,**" Thomas puffed to himself.

It was working.

Thomas was catching up with the plane!

The plane came down to land on an airstrip near the railway tracks.

A little nervously now, Thomas came to a stop beside the plane.

He admired the whirring propeller and the big, red dots painted on its wings.

**"I'm Thomas,"** said Thomas, shyly.

**"I'm Mitchell, the Spitfire,** but you can call me Mitch," the plane replied. "I've been practising for a flypast to celebrate the end of World War II."

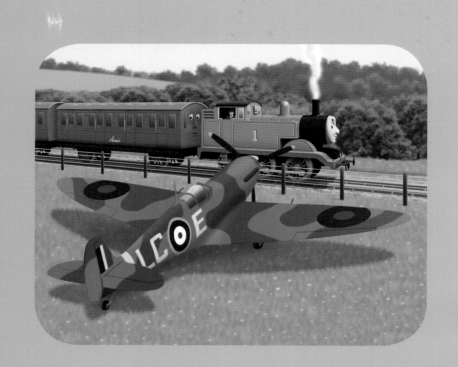

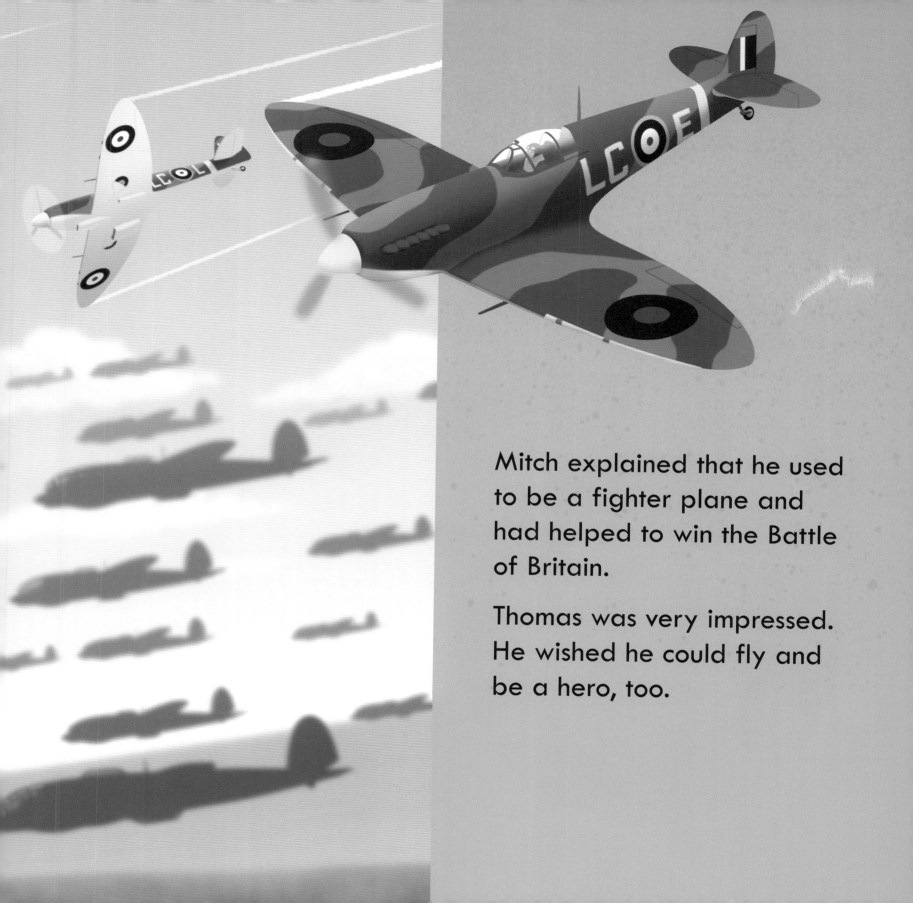

Mitch explained that he used to be a fighter plane and had helped to win the Battle of Britain.

Thomas was very impressed. He wished he could fly and be a hero, too.

Back in the Sheds, Thomas told the other engines about his new friend.

**"Eyes on the tracks, eyes on the tracks,"** they said, crossly.

That night, Thomas' dreams were full of Spitfires diving through the skies. He dreamt that he was flying with them, keeping people safe.

The next day, Thomas was in charge of taking passengers to the airshow for the big flypast.

As he arrived, Thomas could see Mitch and next to him was another vintage plane.

"That's a Hawker Hurricane," Thomas' driver told him. "Hurricanes and Spitfires were the **heroes** of the **Battle of Britain.**"

The show was about to begin ...

The planes revved their engines and rattled along the runway. With just a little **wobble**, they lifted into the sky.

Thomas couldn't resist following them ...

But Mitch seemed to be in trouble. His engine spluttered ... he came lower ... and lower ... and lower until with a big **SPLASH!** he made an emergency landing in a duck pond!

"What shall we do?" asked Mitch, as he started to sink lower and

"I can help, I can help," puffed Thomas,

"It's an emergency," he said as he PUSHED

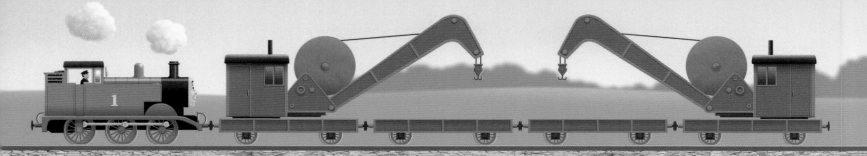

A dripping Mitch was lifted out of the pond.

lower into the muddy pond. "No one will know where I am."

as he hurried back to fetch the breakdown train.

the breakdown train back to Mitch.

The Fat Controller was proud of Thomas.

"Thanks to you, **keeping your eyes on the skies,** you were able to help the Spitfire," he said.

"The planes that took part in the Second World War had to be alert. Like them, you are a **true hero,**" he added.

Thomas was pleased to hear that after a few minor repairs and a new coat of paint Mitch, the Spitfire, was able to take part in many more flypasts. He was even invited to London, where he flew low over the river Thames.

As he looked down at the river, he remembered the time Thomas the hero had rescued him from a very wet landing!

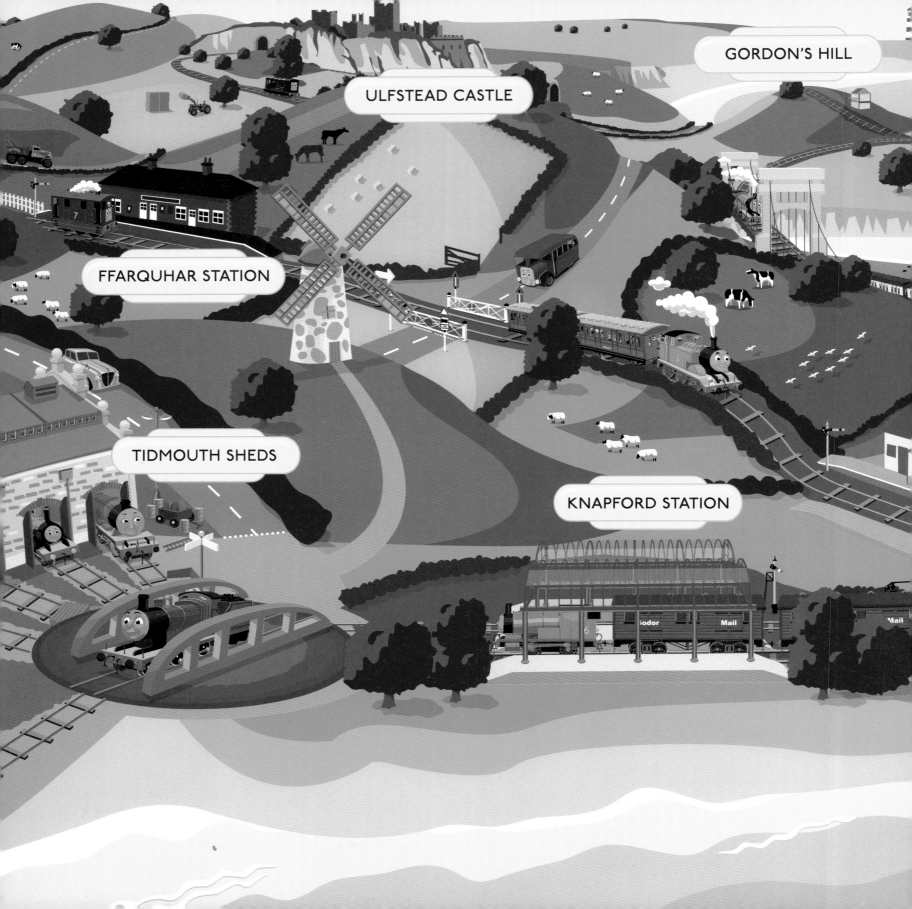

GORDON'S HILL

ULFSTEAD CASTLE

FFARQUHAR STATION

TIDMOUTH SHEDS

KNAPFORD STATION

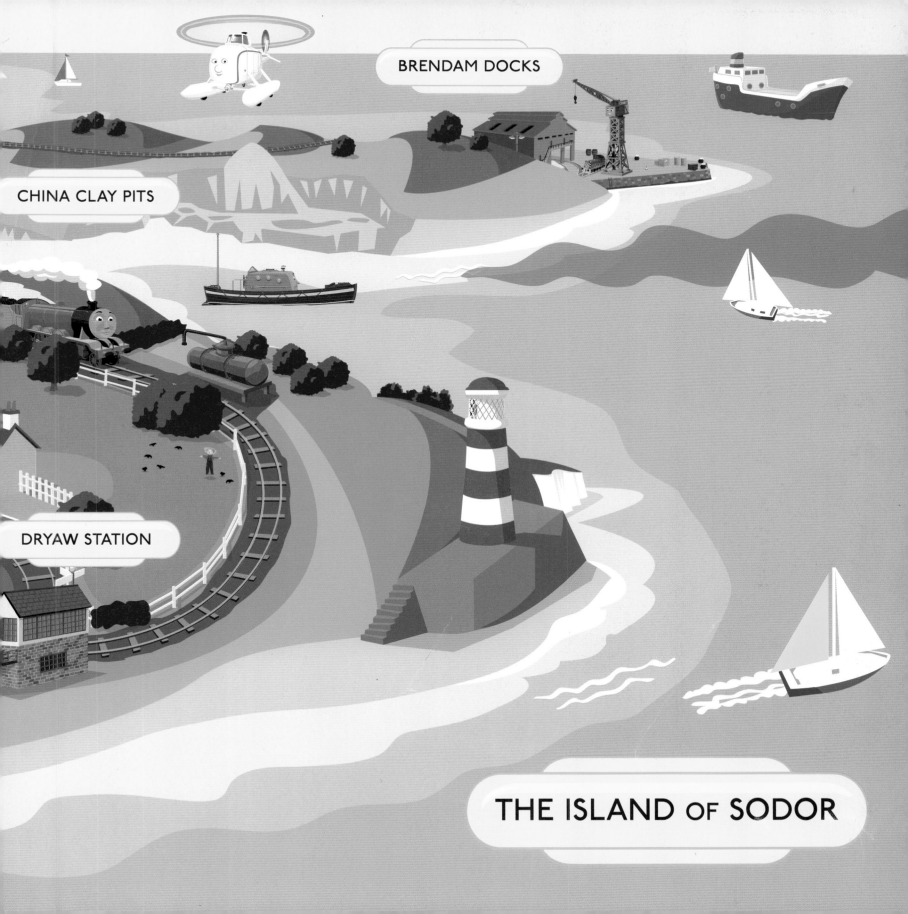

CHINA CLAY PITS

BRENDAM DOCKS

DRYAW STATION

THE ISLAND OF SODOR

# About the author

The Reverend W. Awdry was the creator of 26 little books about Thomas and his famous engine friends, the first being published in 1945. The stories came about when the Reverend's two-year-old son Christopher was ill in bed with the measles. Awdry invented stories to amuse him, which Christopher then asked to hear time and time again. And now, 75 years later, children all around the world continue to be entertained by the Reverend's stories about Thomas, Edward, Gordon, James and the many other Really Useful Engines.

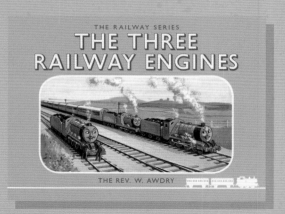

*The Three Railway Engines*, first published in 1945.

The Reverend Awdry with some of his readers at a model railway exhibition.